YESTERDAY'S NEWS – HOT OFF THE PRESS

Dear Reader,

Hello, and welcome to the Egyptian Echo. I'm editor Kanakht and I'm here to tell you that this is the best newspaper on the block!

At the Echo we aim to bring you everything that's fabulous in NEWS and FEATURES. You can see from our contents list that the paper is split into two main sections. First we have news, which takes YOU THE READER through 2,000 years of history. The news comes in three parts, which are the same as the three main eras of Egyptian history – Old Kingdom, Middle Kingdom, and New Kingdom.

Then you've got 13 fascinating pages of features – fashion, pets, dreams, health and the like, all of which remained more or less the same throughout the entire Ancient Egyptian era. Included with that there's our fantastic sphinxational free give-away board game PHARO, that's fun for all the family. Only with the Echo – the paper with a pyramid in its pocket!!

Happy reading readers, and remember –
THE ECHO IS BEST FOR NEWS AND VIEWS!

Kanakht

Editor Kanakht
Egyptian Echo
Pyramid Row
Memphis

THE EGYPTIAN ECHO
was written by
Paul Dowswell
and designed by
Karen Tomlins

With thanks to Charles Freeman, our Ancient Egyptian consultant.

Ian Jackson, Guy Smith, Peter Dennis, Richard Draper, Louise Nixon, Gerald Wood and Robert Walster provided the illustrations.

All photos came from the **Werner Forman Archive, London,** except page 21, bottom; which came from Bildarchiv Foto Marburg. Credit is also due to: British Museum, London (20, 22 middle, 26, 27); Egyptian Museum, Cairo (cover left and right middle, 2, 6 bottom right, 8 top, 21); Louvre Museum, Paris (23); Musees Royaux du Cinquantenaire, Brussels (17, 28); Staatlich Museum, Berlin (15); E. Strouhal (4, 16, 22 top).

EGYPTIAN ECHO ON OTHER PAGES

NARMER NAILS NORTH TO SOUTH

"I'M IN CHARGE" SAYS SCOURGE OF SQUABBLING EGYPT

3100 BC

Tough tribal leaders trembled with terror as King Narmer declared himself ruler of both Upper and Lower Egypt. "I'm in charge now," the former king of Upper Egypt told royal reporters, "and anyone who says I'm not is in BIG TROUBLE."

Not since the Sun god Ra created the world and sent his fellow gods to rule over us has there been such upheaval. For the first time ever the marshlands of the lower Nile Delta and the thin farmlands of the upper Nile Valley are now one country.

Unpleasantness

Despite some general laying waste and other unpleasantness involving death and destruction, most Egyptians are relieved that Narmer has brought to an end centuries of squabbling between these two regions of Egypt.

Cagey

But who is this shadowy figure who has now declared himself "Lord of the Two Lands" and claims to be the gods' representative on Earth? Palace pals are cagey about his true identity. "His mother calls him Narmer," said one, "but he's also known as Menes, and some people even think he's called Aha." When questioned about his

WHO, WHAT AND WHERE

Assorted tribal chiefs in Lower Egypt

MEMPHIS

King Narmer in Upper Egypt

Your at-a-glance guide to who's smiting who.

multiple names a royal spokesman replied, " Narmer, Menes, Aha – call him what you like - just so long as it's 'King of Upper and Lower Egypt'."

Where did you get that hat?

Meanwhile tongues were wagging as fashion watchers predicted a revolutionary new design for the royal crown. Palace insiders have in fact confirmed that Narmer will be combining the conical white crown of Upper Egypt with the red wedge crown of Lower Egypt.

Fashion chiefs were quick to praise the new design. " In a sense," said hat pundit Horem Khauf, " Narmer is quite literally combining his twin roles in one bold statement, and declaring that two hats are better than one, in a very real sense."

Royal wedding due

Narmer's first act as leader of a united Egypt is to set up a capital at Memphis – midway between the two territories. Meanwhile political analysts predict that Narmer will follow a policy of reconciliation with the Delta, marry a Delta princess and attempt to mix lower Egyptian gods and traditions into the culture of Upper Egypt.

You're history, punk! Narmer negotiates his way to a united Egypt. Horus the falcon god helps out.

Proclamation from His Majesty the Pharaoh

Applicants from loyal servants are invited for the following government posts:

Vizier of Upper Egypt
Sole charge of Upper Egypt. Based in Thebes. (Ref. B/45.)

Vizier of Lower Egypt
Sole charge of Lower Egypt. Based in Memphis. (Ref. B/46)

Chief Treasury Official
Must know how many beans make five. Ability to count without use of fingers and toes an advantage. (Ref.B/47)

Chief Granaries Official
Some experience separating wheat from chaff essential. (Ref.B/48)

Chief of Royal Works
Experience of construction projects employing 100,000 or more workers, and almost entire resources of nation would be useful. (Ref. B/49)

Chief Cattle Official
Would suit former farmer. No vegetarians. (Ref. B/50)

Chief Foreign Affairs Official
Multilingual and gestural skills an asset, plus ability to look fierce and uncompromising. (Ref.B/51)

Apply immediately to His most Esteemed and Glorious Majesty the King of Egypt – son of the great god Ra, Royal Palace, Memphis.

The Government of Egypt is not an equal opportunities employer.

IT'S PYRA-MANIA!!

World's greatest wonder unveiled at Giza

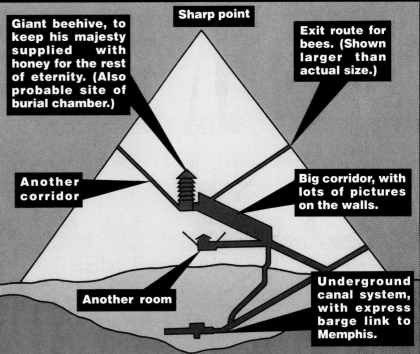

Sharp point

Giant beehive, to keep his majesty supplied with honey for the rest of eternity. (Also probable site of burial chamber.)

Exit route for bees. (Shown larger than actual size.)

Another corridor

Big corridor, with lots of pictures on the walls.

Another room

Underground canal system, with express barge link to Memphis.

The interior of the pyramid is a big secret. However, we have obtained a blueprint. No one's sure what's what, so our expert at the Echo has made a few guesses.

2550 BC

It's Pyramid Week in the Echo, and all of Egypt is going pyramid-crazy! After 20 years of toil and turmoil the Great Pyramid of Pharaoh Khufu is finally finished.

As a team of 100,000 sweating peasants polished up the limestone exterior and cleaned up the debris around the site at Giza, northwest of Memphis, Pharaoh Khufu and his royal entourage went on a regal tour of inspection.

His majesty lingered in the burial chamber at the heart of the pyramid to examine the imposing granite sarcophagus which will be his final resting place.

Ha ha ha!

Turning to royal reporters he declared: "So! My burial monument is ready at last. When I die I shall be safe in the knowledge that my body will be preserved forever in this magnificent structure, and my spirit will ascend to the heavens to take its place among the stars through this stairway to the sky. This is the greatest wonder of all the seven wonders of the world, and it's **mine, all mine**!!! Ha ha ha ha!!!"

Gleaming

Located next to the gleaming white pyramid is a magnificent temple to be used for Khufu's burial service, and within its shadow are lesser tombs awaiting Khufu's family and his many court officials. Competition for a burial spot here is intense, as it is well known that being buried next to the Pharaoh will enable royal insiders to continue to serve their King in his afterlife, and also guarantee them a place in the next world.

Massive

Meanwhile, unconfirmed reports suggest that Khufu's son Khephren is planning an equally massive monument for himself, to be started as soon as he becomes Pharaoh.

But some outsiders are questioning the wisdom of such huge burial monuments. "Just imagine what else the Egyptians could have done with all those resources and manpower," said one Sumerian trader, "like invest it in education. Still, I suppose it keeps them out of mischief!" But Pharaoh Khufu was unconcerned. "Who needs a degree in astronomy to heave a massive slab of granite to the top of my pyramid?" he asked the Echo. "Besides, give a peasant a few qualifications and he starts getting above himself."

CRACKPOT CORNER

You'd think that everyone would know that the Pharaoh is a god and his pyramid is a ladder to help place him among the other gods in the sky. But Egypt's pyramids have provoked all sorts of crackpot theories about what they're here for. Here are just a few of them...

THEORY	THE ECHO SAYS
The pyramids are huge granaries for times of famine.	*Have a bigger breakfast, then you won't be so obsessed with food.*
The angles of internal walls and corridors hold hidden messages about the secrets of the universe.	*Stop reading that papyrus and go out and have some fun.*
Small table-top size paper pyramids have a mystical ability to keep fresh any fruit and milk placed within them. (So do great big pyramids...)	*Here – buy this magic amulet. It's only 12 gold rings, and it's __guaranteed__ to make you irresistibly attractive, unbelievably rich, and immensely popular!*
The pyramids have been built by visitors from another planet.	*We think you've been picking the wrong kind of mushrooms.*

Pyra-facts

Five fascinating pyra-facts about Khufu's pyramid

❶ It's breath-takingly block-tabulous. As many as 2,500,000 limestone and granite blocks have been used in its construction.

❷ Although the limestone comes from local quarries, the granite has been ferried along the Nile from Aswan – 800km (500 miles) away.

❸ It's tun-believably heavy – over 6,000,000 tonnes (tons) in fact.

❹ It's a gigantic compass. The four sides are almost exactly aligned to north, south, east and west.

❺ The outer lime-stone blocks fit so perfectly together it's impossible to insert a knife blade between them.

VOWEL PLAY

"Consonants only" script spells trouble for god of wisdom

Is Thoth a thilly thothage?

Everyone knows that Thoth the god of wisdom gave Egypt the great gift of writing (or "words of the gods" as we Egyptians like to call our beautiful hieroglyphs). Since our history began and scribes first put pen to papyrus, hieroglyphs have been part of Egyptian life.

Here to stay

Without them we wouldn't be able to record the great deeds of our gods and Pharaohs on tombs and monuments. Left to right, right to left, even top to bottom – whichever way you write them, hieroglyphs are here to stay.

Courting controversy, or just plain awkward? Some hieroglyphs, yesterday.

Mithtake

However, some student scribes are daring to whisper that **Thoth hath made a mithtake.** They say hieroglyphs could do with some <u>vowels</u>!

Nebmare nakht, 11, explained.

"Written down, our word for beautiful "nefer" looks like this in hieroglyphs –

– that's "nfr". Why can't we use some symbols for the e sounds, or a, i and u for that matter?"

Dim

"And another thing" piped in Nan Akht, 10, "in the dim and distant future archeologists and explorers from other lands are going to find these things in tombs and monuments and be flummoxed.

They're going to say 'Is it Nufur, Nifir, Nafur or Nefir or what?? Lets call the whole thing off'."

Ears cut off

But scribe school tutors were quick to dismiss their pupils' comments and have punished their impertinence severely. "These two boys have both been beaten to within an inch (26mm) of their lives, in fact they're lucky not to have had their ears cut off," said Scoros Sekhmet, head teacher at the King Khafre School for Scribes.

Don't know they're born

"Besides, I don't know what they're moaning about. There are only 700 characters to learn, and they've got 12 years to learn them in. Young people these days. They don't know they're born."

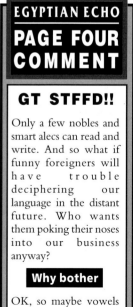

EGYPTIAN ECHO

PAGE FOUR COMMENT

GT STFFD!!

Only a few nobles and smart alecs can read and write. And so what if funny foreigners will have trouble deciphering our language in the distant future. Who wants them poking their noses into our business anyway?

Why bother

OK, so maybe vowels *would* make hieroglyphs easier to read, but who said life was meant to be easy? The **ECHO** says <u>**What you don't know you don't miss!**</u>

Shrug means one million

Any dolt can understand numbers, says mathematician

Mathematicians picked up on the "no vowels" debate yesterday, and have scoffed at scribes and their incredibly complex system of writing. "Nothing can match the simple purity of our wonderful counting system," said top scholar Al Ghebra. "I means one, II means two, III is three, until you get to 10 then it's ∩. That's really easy. When you get to 100 it's a squiggle. 1,000 is a flowery looking thing, and 10,000 is a severed finger. ("Because it just IS," he told a puzzled *Echo* reporter.) 100,000 is some funny furry thing with a tail, and as for one million – it's some bloke going "Pah, I don't know. How do you expect me to count THAT MANY?"

Egyptian counting A beginners guide

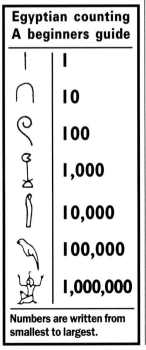

│	I
∩	10
௹	100
𓋹	1,000
𓂭	10,000
𓆐	100,000
𓁨	1,000,000

Numbers are written from smallest to largest.

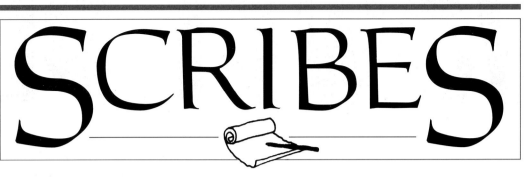

SCRIBES

THAT OUTDATED OLD CLAY SLAB WEIGHING YOU DOWN?

Say goodbye to handwriting misery with Egypt's greatest export – new formula PAPYRUS from *Papco* ©tm

Just compare new formula papyrus with your standard Sumerian clay writing tablet.

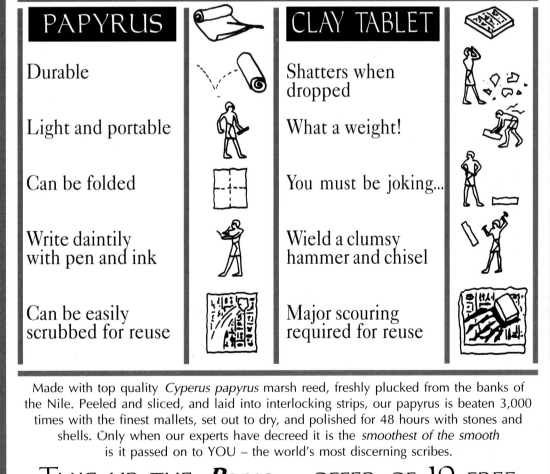

PAPYRUS		CLAY TABLET	
Durable		Shatters when dropped	
Light and portable		What a weight!	
Can be folded		You must be joking...	
Write daintily with pen and ink		Wield a clumsy hammer and chisel	
Can be easily scrubbed for reuse		Major scouring required for reuse	

Made with top quality *Cyperus papyrus* marsh reed, freshly plucked from the banks of the Nile. Peeled and sliced, and laid into interlocking strips, our papyrus is beaten 3,000 times with the finest mallets, set out to dry, and polished for 48 hours with stones and shells. Only when our experts have decreed it is the *smoothest of the smooth* is it passed on to YOU – the world's most discerning scribes.

TAKE UP THE *Papco* ©TM OFFER OF 10 FREE PAPYRUS SHEETS, AND YOU'LL NEVER BUY CLAY TABLETS AGAIN!

KINGDOM CRUMBLES
AS SET TAKES CONTROL

2100 BC

Special report from our calamity and pestilence correspondent Ohdir Whaat–kanthematabe

Despair, destruction, destitution and decay – that's just four things beginning with D they're saying about Egypt today. As I walk through the streets of famine-hit Thebes, this is truly a land where Set the god of disorder has turned the world upside down.

Swagger

Slave girls swagger by decked in gold and silver jewels, noble women weep into their frayed linen dresses, surly children, seeing no future in their life, rebuke their parents saying, "I didn't ask to be born", "I hate you", and "It's not fair."

In a country unused to civil war, starvation and anarchy, these are terrible times.

Feeble

Many I spoke to are quick to blame the situation on the collapse of the pharaoh's power following the especially long reign of Pepi II. After his death rival clans based in Thebes and Herakleopolis are battling for control of the kingdom, and hostile tribes are adding to the chaos by invading from both east and west.

Set – lawless and disordered.

CALAMITY AND PESTILENCE – NOT POPULAR IN EGYPT

Wailing, gnashing of teeth, and major complaining greet the collapse of order in Old Kingdom Egypt.

Man with five names reunites Egypt

2050 BC

Rejoice! Rejoice! That's the word on everyone's lips. Theban prince Mentuhotep II has triumphed over the Herakleopolitan princes, and is set to unite the country and bring to an end 100 years of disorder.

Sweat

Wiping the sweat and dust of battle from his eyes at a hastily convened press conference, Mentuhotep announced, "I intend to unite Egypt and bring to an end 100 years of disorder."

And another thing

"And another thing," he added, "I'm going to build several forts in the desert to make sure the borders are safe from invading tribes, and I'm going to go south to occupy Nubia. This is the beginning of a golden age in Egyptian history. You can't have a golden age without gold, and there's certainly plenty of it down there!"

Mentuhotep – the multi monikered monarch
THOSE OTHER FOUR NAMES IN FULL

S'ankhibtawy	"He who breathes life into the heart of the Two Lands"
Nebhepetre	"The Son of Ra"
Netjerihedjet	"Divine is the white crown"
Sematawy	"He who unifies the Two Lands"

"Mister Chuckle-trousers" is, strangely enough, not one of the many names of Mentuhotep.

6

FEUDING EGYPT FALLS TO FILTHY FOREIGNERS

1660 BC

400 years of peace and prosperity have ended with an invasion. For the first time in its 1600 year history much of the mighty Egyptian nation is under the control of a foreign power.

Taking advantage of a period of decline and feuding with Egypt once again split into two rival dynasties, the Hyksos tribe have swept down from Palestine and overrun the lands of lower Egypt.

Hooligans

The filthy foreign barbarians have been behaving like football hooligans on a drunken weekend and have:

- Burned our cities.
- Razed our temples.
- Been horrible to the locals.
- Set up their own capital in Avaris.
- Made our kings in Thebes pay them taxes.

Not all bad

But some Egyptians insist that the Hyksos aren't all bad. "They do have a tendency to loot and pillage, particularly on a dull Sunday afternoon," said Khon Shotep, a merchant from Buto, "but they like Egypt so much they've adopted our language and culture."

Horse

"And they've brought some very useful things with them," he continued. "They had the novel idea of putting a harness on a horse so that it could pull a chariot. They brought newfangled upright looms, which are much easier to weave cloth on than our old floor looms, and they've introduced new instruments such as lyres and lutes into Egyptian music."

Fortune

But most Egyptians remain unconvinced, and fortune tellers predict some serious smiting awaits the foreign intruders.

Some Hyksos soldiers stealing corn, razing temples and burning cities. The locals don't like them.

HYKSOS HEXPELLED

AHMOSE ON THE LOOSE

1550 BC

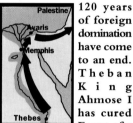

Ahmose's route to victory

120 years of foreign domination have come to an end. Theban King Ahmose I has cured Egypt of a nasty dose of the Hyksosis! The mighty monarch has swept north from his Theban power base to suppress the Hyksos tribe, who had overrun the delta region. The Echo is pleased to report that His Majesty has annihilated the alien intruders.

Uneasy

Upper Egypt has endured an uneasy peace with the foreign invaders, and relations have always been uncomfortable. Not only were the Theban kings **forced** to pay taxes to the Hyksos, but the interlopers **insisted** on venerating Set the god of disorder, AND **complained** about our hippopotami keeping them awake at night with their bellowing.

Domination

In his victory speech Ahmose told reporters, "We've given them a good hiding, and they **won't be back**! Once we've reconquered Nubia nothing will stand in the way of WORLD DOMINATION!!"

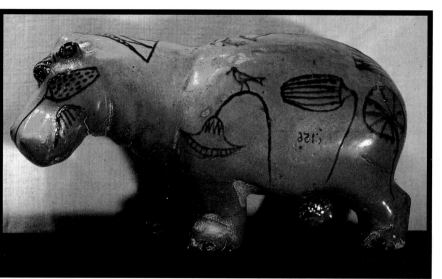
A hippopotamus. A major player in the Egyptian campaign to drive away the Hyksos.

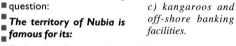
Sex change pharaoh claims dad was a god

1470 BC

Pharaoh Hatshepsut, who has ruled Egypt brilliantly for nearly 20 years, is a WOMAN. And that's not all. She claims her dad is none other than Amun – king of the gods!! So says a secret source from inside the royal circle at Thebes.

Sauce!

The palace insider (whose identity cannot be disclosed for fear of his immediate execution) revealed to the Echo that Hatshepsut, who appears in statues as a man, and is

Hatshepsut yesterday, worrying her pretty little head about affairs of state.

addressed as "His Majesty", is undoubtedly a woman. "It was giving birth to two daughters that really gave the game away," he said.

Polish

The shadowy source, who works in the palace as a crown polisher, agreed to tell all to the Echo for a fee of three goats, four jars of wine, and a baboon.

He went on to reveal that Hatshepsut also maintains that her father is Amun. "Well the story is that the king of the gods was wandering around one day when he saw Mrs. Ahmose, that's Hatshepsut's mother. He was absolutely THUNDERSTRUCK by her beauty. Being a god, like, he didn't mess around, he just disguised himself as Ahmose's actual husband Tuthmosis I. Lucky fellow – that's not a bad trick if you ask my opinion!"

But this **double-shock-horror stunner of a scandal** is unlikely to tarnish Hatshepsut's regal reputation. The Pharaoh has **ruled** with great dignity. She has **restored** many buildings destroyed by the Hyksos, led

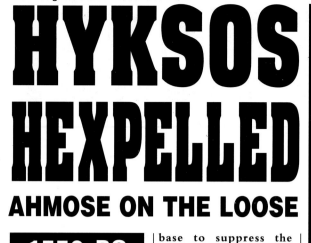
Ma and Pa Hatshepsut, aka Mr. and Mrs. Tuthmosis I.

the Egyptian army into battle in Nubia and the eastern empire, and even sent a **successful trading expedition** to the far off African land of Punt.

PAGE EIGHT COMMENT

Miss is a hit!

Everyone knows that having men as pharaohs is part of the god-given **natural order** of things. Like going to school or being a government official, it is **simply something** a lady should not worry her pretty little head about. However, under the circumstances the Echo has to say: **"Well done Ma'am – NOT BAD FOR A WOMAN!!"**

WE'RE IN THE MONEY
(WELL WE WOULD BE IF IT HAD BEEN INVENTED)

1457 BC

Tuthmosis III, the mightiest of all warrior pharaohs, has added yet <u>another</u> feather to his cap with the defeat of the Mitannian army. The Egyptian Empire is now at its greatest extent EVER.

As trade flourishes, and tribute and taxes pour in from foreign lands, Egypt is set to become IMMENSELY WEALTHY!

Threat

But Tuthmosis's task has not been an easy one. The lands of Canaan (see map), acquired by Tuthmosis's grandfather Tuthmosis I, have been under constant threat from Egypt's two arch eastern rivals, the Hittites and the Mitannians.

Warpath

Tuthmosis III decided the Hits and the Mits needed **STRAIGHTENING OUT**, and has gone on the warpath **17 times** against them.

He **harassed** the Hits who threw in the towel before it came to an out-and-out punch-up, but he had to **mash** the Mits at the battle of Megiddo before they declared "enough is enough".

Couldn't be done

"<u>They</u> said it couldn't be done," he boasted to royal reporters after the battle, "but <u>they</u> were not great men of vision, genius and immense personal charisma – like me." Tuthmosis went on to explain how, against the advice of all his top generals, he had led his army over a steep mountain path, surprised the Mitannian forces from behind, and crushed them utterly.

Coining it in

The successful campaign now leaves Egypt free to enjoy the benefits of its substantial empire. With silver and tin coming in from Canaan, salt and wine from Libya, copper and turquoise from Sinai, gold and slaves from Nubia, and ebony and ivory from Kush, the Echo says <u>Good times are here, and they can only get better</u>!

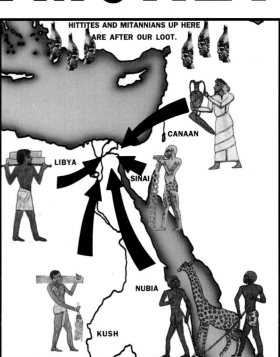

LOOK WHAT WE'VE GOT!! Egypt's greatest ever empire.

TUTHMOSIS III. He had a snake in his hat, rather than a feather.

AKHTOY'S ABODES

44 Sneferu St, Memphis

All sorts of property at prices YOU* can afford!!

Elegant country mansion

Most charming executive 16 room residence, within easy reach of Thebes, so ideal for professional man • Panoramic views of surrounding desert • Traditional unbaked brick construction with stone/wood frames and pillars • Beautifully decorated, with bright floral/geometric designs on plaster • Imposing ramp to substantial "temple style" entrance. Windows placed high in house to minimize penetrating sunlight. (All frames painted in "glare guard" brown paint.) • Bathroom with limestone tub and splash slabs. Toilet with fine stone "keyhole" seat • Magnificent reception room, with matching pillars. Triangular vents on roof to catch refreshing north wind • Own grounds with pool containing water birds • Kitchen on roof. Cool cellar incorporating plentiful water storage facilities (four large jars).

Superb town house

BACK ON MARKET

Individual and most impressive Eighteenth Dynasty town house occupying unique location in heart of Memphis • Would suit royal official • Expansive grounds, with own well. Imposing doorway carved with inscriptions venerating owner • Three floors with 30 rooms in total • Ground floor comprised of baking and cloth-making area open to courtyard • Principal floor comprised of impressive main reception room with brilliant blue ceiling, and living quarters for family • Master bedroom with adjoining bathroom and brick/wood "seat style" toilet with pot and sand container • Top floor comprised of office/living quarters. Each room complete with beautifully painted columns • Flat roof suitable for cooking area, and sleeping space for servants.

Worker's cottage

Delightful terraced dwelling built within safety of walled village • Mud construction. Near to fields. Plain "peasant fashion" mud walls, incorporating multiple niches for placement of statues to household gods • Thatch roof (with openings for light and ventilation) • Feature raised brick bed, in main bedroom. Cellar offering walk-in storage facility, set beneath earth style floor.

Character two-room hovel

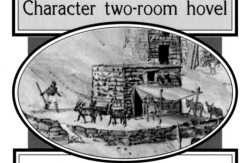

Ideal first-time purchase on outskirts of Memphis • Two rooms with own internal wall (disintegrating) • Close proximity to Nile (prone to flooding). Part covered "open access" roof, giving generous light and ventilation • Near small stream for bathing, and close-by handy field with several bushes (non-prickly) for "other purposes". Healthy "good for you" style trek to nearest well.

Traditional town house

BARGAIN OF THE WEEK

Most sought-after premier residential location, enjoying benefits of bustling downtown Sais • Strong, unbaked brick construction will allow building of additional level on roof • Bedroom with semi-private partition – ideal for portable toilet • Opportunity for expansion, as several adjacent properties are derelict.

Akhtoy's descriptions of appliances/services or indeed entire residences should not be taken as a guarantee that these items are in working order, or even exist. We recommend that purchasers arrange for a qualified scribe to check these dwellings thoroughly.

*Depending on who you are.

SUN SETS ON "SON OF SUN"

Light goes out on Akhenaten

Akhenaten. He liked the sun and art, but lost control of Syria.

1336 BC

Akhenaten, the maverick pharaoh who venerated the sun and declared war on all the other gods of Egypt, <u>is dead</u>.

But even as the royal corpse grows cold, and the nation prepares to bury the most unconventional monarch in its history, political pundits are arguing over the merits of his rule.

"Akhenaten cast several very large boulders into the placid lotus pond of Egyptian society, and the waves they made have created unheard of upheaval in a hitherto changeless land," said the Echo's royal correspondent shortly before the editor said, "You're fired".

Amen to Aten

Akhenaten came to the throne as Amenhoptep IV in 1352. But the sun-crazy sovereign took a new name – meaning *pious servant of Aten* – six years into his reign. Although he ruled over a land of many gods, Akhenaten became convinced that there was only one god – and that god was the **SUN ITSELF** – known as **THE ATEN**.

Sunstroke

Egyptians wondered if their pharaoh was suffering from sunstroke, as Akhenaten declared:

• The sun was his **FATHER**.
• **ONLY AKHENATEN** and his family could worship The Aten – everyone else had to worship Akhenaten.
• Worship of all other gods was **FORBIDDEN**.
• The great temples of Amun, king of the gods, were to be **SHUT DOWN**.
• Statues of all other gods were to be **SMASHED**, and their names **REMOVED** from all statues and monuments.
• Homage was to be paid to The Aten in large courtyards **OPEN TO THE SKY**, and filled with altars where devotees could place fruits and flowers and other bountiful products of the sun.

Rival

But sunstroke may not have been the sole reason for these changes. Political observers are suggesting that Akhenaten promoted the worship of the sun because he feared that temples to the god Amun were becoming so rich and powerful that they competed with the pharaoh himself for control of the land.

So what

Yet despite the revolutionary nature of these changes the average Egyptian in the street was more than likely untouched by Akhenaten's new religion. Compared to the usual gods of Egypt the sun was faceless and characterless.

Most Egyptians have little shrines to their gods at home, and continued to worship at them, no matter what Akhenaten said.

THE REVOLUTIONARY RULER'S REGAL RECORD

Four <u>other</u> things Akhenaten did, apart from insisting everyone worship The Aten.

① Built a luxurious new capital called Akhetaten, midway between Memphis and Thebes.

② Lost control of the colony Egypt had established in Syria, which was taken over by the Hittites.

③ Married Nefertiti, said to be one of the most beautiful women in the world. (However, some gossips say that a shadow fell over their relationship, and she squabbled with Akhenaten before she died.)

Nefertiti

④ Encouraged artists to paint sweeping, graceful images full of life and movement, rather than stiff and stilted depictions of the items they portrayed.

Unforgettable – that's what you aren't

A palace scribe erasing all mention of Akhenaten from royal records.

HOREMHEB SET TO TURN AKHENATEN INTO INVISIBLE MAN

1320 BC

Pharaoh Horemheb has turned the tables on the most table-turning, topsy-turvy, back-to-front, upside-down pharaoh in history.

The former general turned monarch has told reporters he intends to wipe the name of Pharaoh Akhenaten <u>from the very pages of history!!</u> "Akhenaten tried to stamp out our gods, so now we're going to **STAMP HIM OUT**. Henceforth it will be forbidden to speak his name out loud, and he shall only be known as *that criminal*. All his statues and every inscription of his name shall be **UTTERLY ERADICATED**. All temples to his god, The Aten, are to be closed <u>AT ONCE</u> and then torn down."

Tut tut

He went on " Much of the harm caused by *that criminal* has been undone during the reign of my predecessor King Tut. Worship of the old gods has been restored, and the capital moved from Akhetaten back to Memphis. But I intend to erase his name from all records, and <u>it's going to be like he never existed</u>."

Godless? You need...

12 *The publishers consider full reproduction of these particular deities unsuitable for a family newspaper.

SUPERPOWER STALEMATE ends in treaty

Ram and Hat say let's be pals

1268 BC

Egypt's arch rivals the Hittites woke up this morning to discover they are now our BEST FRIENDS. Pharaoh Ramesses II has signed the first state-to-state peace treaty in history with former foe and top Hittite Hattusilis III.

Silver

The treaty, which is engraved on a silver tablet, sets out several ground-breaking agreements between the Egyptians and Hittites. Among them are reassurances that:

• *We promise not to* **pinch** *their territory if they promise not to pinch ours.*
• *There'll be no more* **jabbing, slugging and smiting** *between us (no hostilities at all in fact, although hitting with pillows, tickling, and making mildly impudent remarks about each other are still allowed).*
• *We'll* **support** *each other if anyone else attacks us, no matter how big they are.*
• *Political rivals of Ramesses and Hattusilis will not be offered* **refuge** *in each other's country.*
• *Ramesses is to* **marry** *one of Hattusilis's daughters.*

Decades

The treaty ends decades of rivalry between the two great Middle East superpowers. Political observers attribute their willingness to compromise on the need to defend themselves from other nations in the region.

"There are too many other blood lusting, power hungry, land chomping, gold grubbing nations like the Syrians, Babylonians and Libyans out there for them to cope with," said Scholar Mengebet, of the Memphis Institute for Strategic Studies, Tactical Teaching and Military Methodology. (M.I.S.S.T.T.M.M. for short).

More temples

But whatever the reason, Ramesses II will now have more time and energy to spend on his great passion – BUILDING TEMPLES.

Reckless archers from the Ptah division shoot arrows into the air to celebrate the fact that we're now pals with the Hittites.

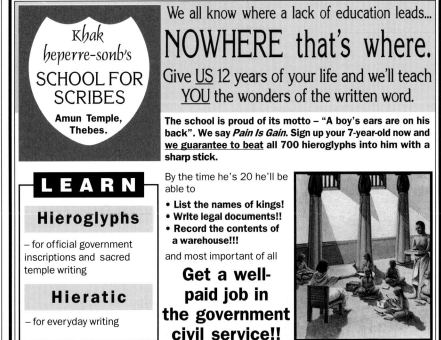

SEA PEOPLE SCUTTLED
RAMESSES III DIVES IN WITH BOTH FISTS FLYING

1174 BC

Ramesses III's reputation as the guardian angel of Egypt has been sealed. Front line dispatches from the Nile Delta have confirmed that he has won a decisive naval battle against the latest in a long line of invading barbarians – the so-called Sea People.

Motley

For many years this motley alliance of miscellaneous Mediterraneans has been creeping toward our shores, intent on conquest, not to mention plundering and looting. Rampant Ramesses reacted with righteous wrath when their invasion fleet reached the Nile Delta. He wreaked havoc on the Mediterranean marauders, assisted by an army battle-hardened by his recent campaigns against invading Libyans. **The Sea People have been decisively splashed, ducked, held under water, and buried up to their necks in sand.**

Serious

The Sea People threat has been serious enough for every single Egyptian male of military age to be called into service. Ramesses told reporters, "These Sea People,

they're the Hyksos of the 1170s – settling wherever they like, and pillaging as they go. They've been on the warpath since Amenhotep III was a lad★, and they're not coming here, I can tell you."

★ *Note for scholars – c.1400BC*

Loyal

His loyal subjects were quick to praise their fiery king's briny show of belligerent brilliance, but seemed to be weary of the constant struggle to keep Egypt free from raiders and invaders. "Wars, we're ★★★★★★★ sick of them," said Meket aten, a chariot driver from Thebes. "If it's not the ★★★★★★★ Libyans invading us, it's these ★★★★★★★ Sea People. I'd hang them up by their ankles and throw crocodiles at them, if you ask me."

Ramesses in outright termination mode. His "no-nonsense" approach won the day.

Ramesses on the rampage.

ALL OUT STRIKE!

Wageless workers in wildcat walk-out

Workers' spokesman Ptah-emdjehuty claims he's starving.

1150 BC

The nation is reeling from the news that workers building the tomb of mighty warrior Ramesses III have GONE ON STRIKE.

In a shock move unprecedented in the Egyptian construction industry, the royal tomb craftsmen downed tools when their wages failed to arrive for the **second month running**.

Grain drain

"We get paid in goods and food," said workers' spokesman Ptah-emdjehuty, "and we're not doing any more work 'til we get some."

As he spoke an angry loin-cloth clothed mob gathered outside the half-completed tomb and began to chant:
"What do we want? – Grain, oil and linen, and a little bit of silver on special occasions!"
"When do we want it? – NOW, or as soon as Ramesses sees fit – but he'd better hurry up because we're starving!"

Fabric

Palace spokesman Vizier Ta was quick to condemn the striking workers, and blamed their lack of wages on a nationwide shortage of grain. "These people are politically motivated shirkers," he told the Echo. "The very fabric of the nation is decaying. The conscience of the population is withering"

Plot

The strike is indeed further evidence of the decline of Egyptian civilization. Despite brilliant military victories, the reign of Ramesses III has seen escalating price rises, disrupted trade, dishonest incompetent government, and even a plot to assassinate the King himself.

COURT REPORT

Brought to you by Ma'at, the goddess of

JUSTICE & TRUTH

Headhunting boss nose best

Top estate official Nakht Sobk has had his nose cut off after a court at Abydos found him guilty of kidnapping a herdsman belonging to a rival estate. Sobk seized the man (who has not been named) because he was impressed by his sheepherding abilities. "You can't get good staff these days," he told the court. "So I told him he was being headhunted."

But neither the herdsman nor Judge Neferhotep was impressed by this line of argument. "The law is quite clear on this point," the judge told Sobk. "*If any man shall seize a herdsman and cause him to say 'ruin has befallen my cattle', then he shall be beaten with 200 blows and have his nose cut off.* Your exemplary record as a good citizen has saved you from the beating, but your lack of nose will serve as a permanent reminder that high officials cannot do just what they wish."

The Echo court artist's dramatic depiction of Sobk's trial. The estate official (waving arms) pleads for his nose.

Tool thief DEATH DRAMA

A Theban woman has been sentenced to death after a workers' court found her guilty of stealing tools from a fellow worker. The woman, known only as Herya, swore an oath in court protesting her innocence before the god Amun, and the Pharaoh himself. She did look silly, when shortly thereafter, a court official dispatched to her house dug up the very tools in question.

Worker-magistrate Henut Kagab was unequivocal in his sentence. "Exceedingly guilty is the citizeness Herya, and worthy of death." However, the workers' court does not have the power to carry out a death sentence, and Herya's case is to be heard by Vizier Kentika.

WORKERS IN CURSE OUTRAGE

Foreman Nemty Nakht is alleging that four of his workers spoke blasphemously against the Pharaoh. "I clearly heard one of these men say 'Pharaoh has a nose like a jackal and the character of a cantankerous baboon'," Nakht told the Theban workers' court.

He went on "Another said '... and he stinks like a jackal after a four week trek through the baking desert.' Then they all snickered like naughty student scribes."

The four workers deny the allegations, which, if proven, could result in their execution. They say they had recently discovered that Nakht had been illegally bartering granite building blocks for shipments of wine and ostrich feathers, and that he is trying to frame them.

The case continues.

RED FACES FOR TOE TORTURE TOMB ROBBERS

A Theban court heard yesterday how two peasants on a tomb robbing rampage had red faces when they went to sleep " on the job", and were caught red-handed.

Imhotep Intef and Itruri Kagab broke into the tomb of Bakenptah Amenhotep in Abydos. After a hard afternoon ransacking, plundering, looting and despoiling, they fell upon the food and wine Amenhotep's devoted wife Akh-menu had left to nourish his spirit, and gobbled down the lot.

Feeling tired, they decided to lie down for a while before they moved on. Tomb guards, alerted by what they described as "low rumbling noises" coming from within the tomb, moved in and made a swift arrest.

Feet

Judge Nebre was merciless with the men. "Tomb robbery is one of the great curses of the modern world," he told them. "Your guilt is established beyond all doubt. I sentence you to have your feet beaten with a big stick."

Intef and Kagab await their turn before Judge Nebre with other miscreants at the Theban court.

Hide-and-seek

Three thieves who stole 20 cattle hides from a tannery have been arrested and punished with a beating of 100 blows and five large cuts.

Judge Kanakht told the men, "God knows the wrongdoer, and punishes his sin with blood. Be thankful I have not ordered your ears to be cut off."

"District Five" face Vizier Kentika

Five district governors are being tried by Pharaoh's deputy, Vizier Kentika, in the highest court in the land. They face charges of withholding taxes, taking bribes, and failing to assess local estates. If found guilty the five face a life-threatening beating of 200 blows, and social and professional disgrace.

"Donkeys ate my taxes" pleads peasant

Ammun Enshi, a peasant from Selima, has been given a swift beating with a stick for late payment of taxes. Judge Anubis heard that Enshi had been unable to pay his taxes after a herd of donkeys ate half his corn crop. "Your misfortune has saved you from further punishment," the judge told Enshi. "But if you are unable to pay your taxes again, you will be conscripted into the Karnak temple building project."

Enshi is given a short, sharp shock. "It's disgraceful," says his mother.

Don't spill that salt or break that mirror, and definitely don't go walking under any ladders – it's

PESHED'S PROSPECTS

Greetings, O readers. I, Peshed, the Echo's oracular prophet of good days, bad days, and auspicious and inauspicious portents bring you news of the FUTURE.

The season of Akhet* is upon us, and here is my forecast for the next 120 days.

The 26th – a good day for ducks.

The first month of Akhet

The **26th day of the month** is a **hostile** day. It is the day when Horus the great protector, and Set the god of disorder, declared war upon each other and brought chaos and woe to the world.

Do not go out of doors between dusk and dawn, as great misfortune will befall you. Between dawn and dusk you may go about your business providing you do not partake in any of the following activities: bathing, boating, making a journey, eating fish or any other water-living creature, killing a goat, ox or duck, lighting a fire in the house, and listening to cheerful songs.

You are also forewarned that uttering the name of Set, the god of disorder, will ensure that your house **will never be free of squabbling and ill temper**.

The 6th – don't drink barley beer.

The second month of Akhet

I have much news for those who were born in this month.

Those born on the **fourth day of the month**. You are likely to die of fever. Always take a cloak when you go out, in case it rains and you catch a chill.

Those born on the **fifth day of the month**. You are likely to die of a broken heart. Perhaps you could become a hermit, and go and live on your own at the top of a mountain.

Those born on the **sixth day of the month**. You are likely to die of drink. Stay away from that barley beer if you can possibly help it.

Those born on the **ninth day of the month**. Congratulations, you are likely to die of old age. Make sure you have plenty of children, so at least some of the ingrates will be around to look after you when you are an old codger.

Those born on the **23rd day of the month**. Snap, crunch, chomp. Watch out for crocodiles!!

Those born on the **27th day of the month**. Hsssssssss. Watch out for snakes!!

Those born on the **29th day of the month**. Your life will be much blessed and when you die you will be a highly respected gentleman, your worship, sir.

A local temple, yesterday.

The third month of Akhet

Peshed regrets to announce that he has no predictions for this month. Please consult your local temple oracle for details.

The 28th - 30th. Get planting!

The fourth month of Akhet

The **28th, 29th and 30th days of the month** are **good days**. On these days Horus and Set called an end to their struggle, and peace fell upon the world. These are good days to wage war against the enemies of Egypt, and on a more mundane level, to sow crops or begin to cultivate a piece of land.

---

*Note to foreigners. The Egyptian year is divided into three seasons – Akhet, when the Nile floods its banks (July to October), Peret, when the waters recede (November to February) and Shemu, the time of harvest (March to June). There are four thirty-day months in each season.

SOCKS CRISIS

1300 BC

• 2,000 years of mainly uninterrupted peace and prosperity.

• The most extraordinary buildings in the world, EVER.

• Fantastic craftsmen and architects that make other nations green with envy.

• A system of government which usually stays in power by looking after its people – rather than hitting them regularly with a big stick.

We've had it all. **But are we going to be able to keep it?**

BURST

The Egyptian nation has had several great advantages over its rivals. Since the dawn of time the Nile river has burst its banks every July and poured fertilizing silt over the fields. When the waters recede we get to plant and harvest record-breaking crops. Since King Narmer united the region way back in 3100BC, we've made the most of this regular supply of food and built a **prosperous, ordered world** where government ruled, and craftsmen flourished. Being surrounded by sea and desert meant invasion by greedy outsiders was all but **impossible**.

ALL CHANGE

BUT THIS HAS ALL CHANGED. The Sahara Desert is getting **dryer**. In the west, wandering tribes from Libya are desperate to settle in our fertile land, **and they don't mind waving their swords around to do so**. Mediterranean and Asian armies are pouring in from the east, all itching to get their hands on **our** wealth.

ROTTEN RULERS

We've been telling them to get lost for twenty centuries – **so why worry now?** Because 50 years of **weak rulers** have led to a **crumbling** respect for the Pharaoh and the power he represents. **Corrupt** government officials are squandering Egypt's wealth. Squabbling Mediterranean powers have **disrupted** our great trading empire. The goldmines of Nubia are all **exhausted**. In the midst of all this the **threat** to our country from outsiders has never been **greater** – yet we've never been **less able** to resist it.

The Echo says the barbarians are at the gates. LET'S PULL OUR SOCKS UP – BEFORE IT'S TOO LATE.

PHARO

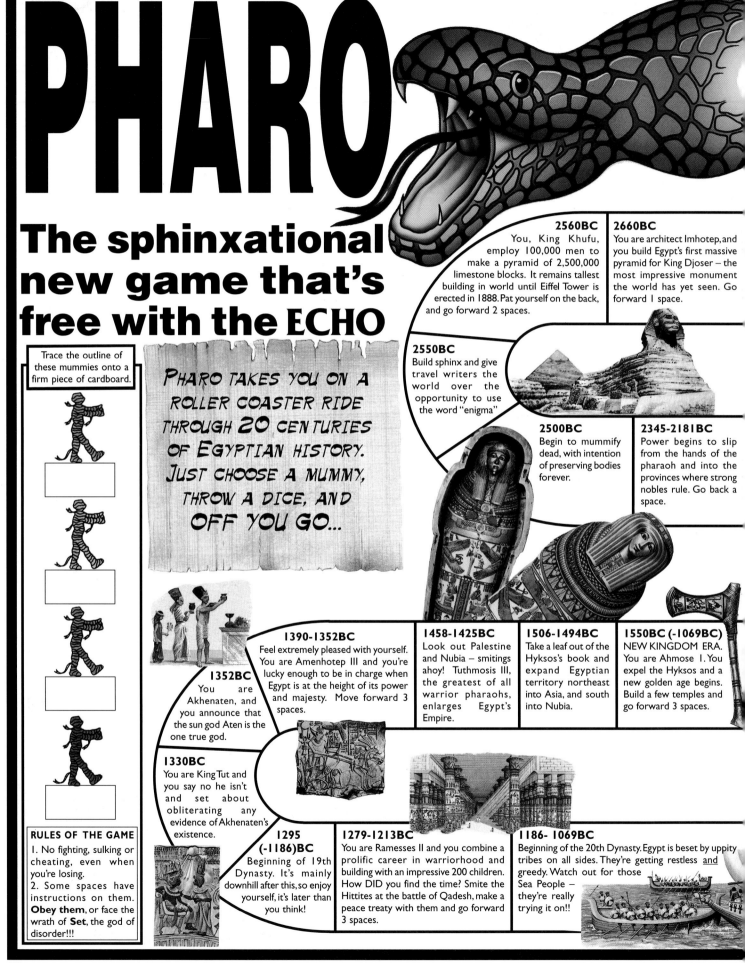

The sphinxational new game that's free with the ECHO

Trace the outline of these mummies onto a firm piece of cardboard.

PHARO TAKES YOU ON A ROLLER COASTER RIDE THROUGH 20 CENTURIES OF EGYPTIAN HISTORY. JUST CHOOSE A MUMMY, THROW A DICE, AND OFF YOU GO...

2660BC
You are architect Imhotep, and you build Egypt's first massive pyramid for King Djoser – the most impressive monument the world has yet seen. Go forward 1 space.

2560BC
You, King Khufu, employ 100,000 men to make a pyramid of 2,500,000 limestone blocks. It remains tallest building in world until Eiffel Tower is erected in 1888. Pat yourself on the back, and go forward 2 spaces.

2550BC
Build sphinx and give travel writers the world over the opportunity to use the word "enigma"

2500BC
Begin to mummify dead, with intention of preserving bodies forever.

2345-2181BC
Power begins to slip from the hands of the pharaoh and into the provinces where strong nobles rule. Go back a space.

1550BC (-1069BC)
NEW KINGDOM ERA. You are Ahmose I. You expel the Hyksos and a new golden age begins. Build a few temples and go forward 3 spaces.

1506-1494BC
Take a leaf out of the Hyksos's book and expand Egyptian territory northeast into Asia, and south into Nubia.

1458-1425BC
Look out Palestine and Nubia – smitings ahoy! Tuthmosis III, the greatest of all warrior pharaohs, enlarges Egypt's Empire.

1390-1352BC
Feel extremely pleased with yourself. You are Amenhotep III and you're lucky enough to be in charge when Egypt is at the height of its power and majesty. Move forward 3 spaces.

1352BC
You are Akhenaten, and you announce that the sun god Aten is the one true god.

1330BC
You are King Tut and you say no he isn't and set about obliterating any evidence of Akhenaten's existence.

1295 (-1186)BC
Beginning of 19th Dynasty. It's mainly downhill after this, so enjoy yourself, it's later than you think!

1279-1213BC
You are Ramesses II and you combine a prolific career in warriorhood and building with an impressive 200 children. How DID you find the time? Smite the Hittites at the battle of Qadesh, make a peace treaty with them and go forward 3 spaces.

1186- 1069BC
Beginning of the 20th Dynasty. Egypt is beset by uppity tribes on all sides. They're getting restless <u>and</u> greedy. Watch out for those Sea People – they're really trying it on!!

RULES OF THE GAME
1. No fighting, sulking or cheating, even when you're losing.
2. Some spaces have instructions on them. **Obey them**, or face the wrath of **Set**, the god of disorder!!!

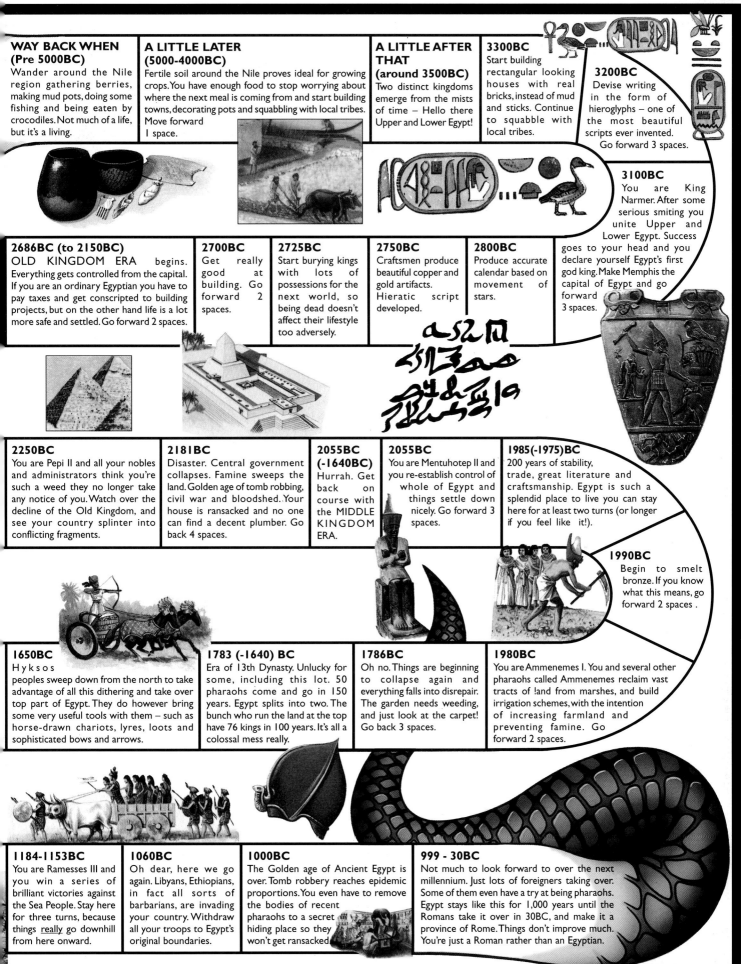

WAY BACK WHEN (Pre 5000BC)

Wander around the Nile region gathering berries, making mud pots, doing some fishing and being eaten by crocodiles. Not much of a life, but it's a living.

A LITTLE LATER (5000-4000BC)

Fertile soil around the Nile proves ideal for growing crops. You have enough food to stop worrying about where the next meal is coming from and start building towns, decorating pots and squabbling with local tribes. Move forward 1 space.

A LITTLE AFTER THAT (around 3500BC)

Two distinct kingdoms emerge from the mists of time – Hello there Upper and Lower Egypt!

3300BC

Start building rectangular looking houses with real bricks, instead of mud and sticks. Continue to squabble with local tribes.

3200BC

Devise writing in the form of hieroglyphs – one of the most beautiful scripts ever invented. Go forward 3 spaces.

3100BC

You are King Narmer. After some serious smiting you unite Upper and Lower Egypt. Success goes to your head and you declare yourself Egypt's first god king. Make Memphis the capital of Egypt and go forward 3 spaces.

2686BC (to 2150BC)

OLD KINGDOM ERA begins. Everything gets controlled from the capital. If you are an ordinary Egyptian you have to pay taxes and get conscripted to building projects, but on the other hand life is a lot more safe and settled. Go forward 2 spaces.

2700BC

Get really good at building. Go forward 2 spaces.

2725BC

Start burying kings with lots of possessions for the next world, so being dead doesn't affect their lifestyle too adversely.

2750BC

Craftsmen produce beautiful copper and gold artifacts. Hieratic script developed.

2800BC

Produce accurate calendar based on movement of stars.

2250BC

You are Pepi II and all your nobles and administrators think you're such a weed they no longer take any notice of you. Watch over the decline of the Old Kingdom, and see your country splinter into conflicting fragments.

2181BC

Disaster. Central government collapses. Famine sweeps the land. Golden age of tomb robbing, civil war and bloodshed. Your house is ransacked and no one can find a decent plumber. Go back 4 spaces.

2055BC (-1640BC)

Hurrah. Get back on course with the MIDDLE KINGDOM ERA.

2055BC

You are Mentuhotep II and you re-establish control of whole of Egypt and things settle down nicely. Go forward 3 spaces.

1985(-1975)BC

200 years of stability, trade, great literature and craftsmanship. Egypt is such a splendid place to live you can stay here for at least two turns (or longer if you feel like it!).

1990BC

Begin to smelt bronze. If you know what this means, go forward 2 spaces.

1650BC

Hyksos peoples sweep down from the north to take advantage of all this dithering and take over top part of Egypt. They do however bring some very useful tools with them – such as horse-drawn chariots, lyres, loots and sophisticated bows and arrows.

1783 (-1640) BC

Era of 13th Dynasty. Unlucky for some, including this lot. 50 pharaohs come and go in 150 years. Egypt splits into two. The bunch who run the land at the top have 76 kings in 100 years. It's all a colossal mess really.

1786BC

Oh no. Things are beginning to collapse again and everything falls into disrepair. The garden needs weeding, and just look at the carpet! Go back 3 spaces.

1980BC

You are Ammenemes I. You and several other pharaohs called Ammenemes reclaim vast tracts of land from marshes, and build irrigation schemes, with the intention of increasing farmland and preventing famine. Go forward 2 spaces.

1184-1153BC

You are Ramesses III and you win a series of brilliant victories against the Sea People. Stay here for three turns, because things really go downhill from here onward.

1060BC

Oh dear, here we go again. Libyans, Ethiopians, in fact all sorts of barbarians, are invading your country. Withdraw all your troops to Egypt's original boundaries.

1000BC

The Golden age of Ancient Egypt is over. Tomb robbery reaches epidemic proportions. You even have to remove the bodies of recent pharaohs to a secret hiding place so they won't get ransacked.

999 - 30BC

Not much to look forward to over the next millennium. Just lots of foreigners taking over. Some of them even have a try at being pharaohs. Egypt stays like this for 1,000 years until the Romans take it over in 30BC, and make it a province of Rome. Things don't improve much. You're just a Roman rather than an Egyptian.

Bata's beauty spot

Hot tips from the hottest lips in Memphis!

Hello girls! Bata here with another dispatch from the front line of the Echo's campaign to KEEP EGYPT BEAUTIFUL! So wiggle those hips, flutter those eyelids and LET'S GET GORGEOUS!!

Hair today... shorn tomorrow

Judging by your letters many of you are concerned about greying and thinning hair. A woman's lustrous black mane is her crowning glory and it's important to keep it looking attractive AT ALL TIMES.

For greying hair *a dark and mysterious mixture of black cow blood, black snake fat and raven's eggs will return your tresses to their former glory.*

Thinning hair *is more of a problem, but a preparation*

of mashed up fenugreek seeds rubbed well into the scalp has been known to slow the process down.

The mane attraction. The first step to all-round beauty.

AS SWEET AS YOU ARE

Keep sweet in the baking heat with a deodorant preparation of myrrh, desert date seeds or frankincense, mixed together with the fatty oil of your choice. Incidentally, I'm often asked by noble ladies

why peasants stink so much. The sad truth is that many Egyptians have never seen the inside of a bathroom, and can't afford the expense of keeping clean. Still, let's be thankful some of us can.

KOHLS FROM NUBIA

We've been wearing mesdemet (also known as kohl) as eye shadow since it was first brought back from our lands in Nubia. But did you know that not only does this magnificent black mineral make our eyes look dazzling, it also protects them? Lead sulphide, the main ingredient, acts as a disinfectant, keeps away the flies, and shields our eyes from the sun.

I spy with my little eye, something beginning with 𓏏.

TOP FASHION

Dress to impress – King Tut style

Fortune tellers predict that in the distant future people will say "Clothes maketh the man," and for sure, none of us on the Echo would disagree with THAT!

Tut's top tips

A cloth around the loins might be all right for your run-of-the-mill farm hand, but connoisseurs of true style know that power and respect go hand in hand with a good tailor and jewel maker.

So here, with the help of our own teenage King Tut and his Queen, is the Echo's own guide for the top Egyptian after top marks in the style stakes.

FOR HIM

Clothes that say "I'm in charge"

Sandals – immaculate, gold plated, extremely uncomfortable. These shoes shout "I go everywhere by chariot."

Add instant authority with an elaborate crown. This hat does a lot more than keep the sun off your head!

The ever popular his 'n' hers wide gold collar, with precious jewels. The accessory that screams "I'VE GOT CASH COMING OUT OF MY EARS!!" Wear it plain, or with serpent, vulture or hawk head attachment, in fact any creature that inspires fear and respect will do. (Fashion hint: cow and sheep attachment not recommended.)

Refreshing body oils to keep you cool.

Jewels by Nofret's Nik-naks, Memphis. Clothes by Faras Dwat, Giza. Throne – model's own.

FOR HER

Clothes that declare "I'm the daintiest doll in Upper Egypt"

White linen dress – timeless, elegant simplicity.

Braided wig on shaven head. Say goodbye to headlice misery. Gold tube braiding optional.

Jewel charms to ward off jealous spells and curses that are sure to be winging their way toward anyone as gorgeous as YOU!

Seductive peacock-feather headdress.

Stay feminine, fresh and flagrantly fragrant with sweet lily oil, even in the scorching sun.

Broad gold bracelet. A <u>must</u> – especially if it's a gift from someone even more important than you.

Do tell me madam, why is it that women as beautiful as yourself also seem to be blessed with such style and elegance?

Yes, people tell me I make even Queen Nefertiti look like a hippopotamus!

Well! This is **much** more interesting than talking about my husband.

DREAMS
What do they really mean?

"I had a funny dream last night." Was there ever a conversational gambit more likely to make your eyes glaze over? Let's face it, other people's dreams are really boring, but your own, well, they're really fascinating!

Dreams. We all have them, but what do they really mean? Many people believe that they are one way the gods use to talk to us on Earth. People also believe our dreams show us what lies in the future.

Dream team

Here's a quiz compiled by Echo dream correspondent Tash Khakty and top dream consultant Saq Neferti. See if you can guess the correct interpretation of these dreams, then check your answers to see what your dream interpretation says about YOU!

Dream one

I was standing under a waterfall which was pouring into a crystal clear river, and the water felt really clean and cold.

Meaning:

a) My roof is leaking and the water is pouring over me as I sleep.
b) The gods are smiling on me, and purifying me from all evil.
c) I haven't had a bath for ages, and I feel guilty about it.

Dream two

I was out in the fields and this absolutely massive cat appeared and stared at me for ages.

Meaning:

a) My cat has come into my bedroom and curled up on my head.
b) The gods are smiling on me and there is going to be a really big harvest.
c) A tom cat's been in here and sprayed on my pillow.

Dream three

I was with this really gorgeous man/woman (delete where not applicable), and we were kissing and canoodling and all that.

Meaning:

a) Heavens. It's Mr./Mrs. Hekhbet! Hmm, he/she always was rather cute!
b) The gods are angry with me and I will soon lose a close relative.
c) I was with this really gorgeous man/woman, and we were kissing and canoodling and all that.

Dream four

I was standing in the street, and this huge ostrich ran up to me and we tried to stare each other out.

Meaning:

a) My pillow is stuffed with ostrich feathers.
b) The gods are angry with me and misfortune will soon befall me.
c) Lanky cousin Mekmer is coming to stay. We can't stand each other!

Dream five

I was on this farm and feeding a herd of cattle and they were all mooing and everything.

Meaning:

a) I knew we shouldn't have bought a house too near to Farmer Senini's cow shed.
b) The gods are angry with me and my future is to wander the Earth aimlessly with no direction.
c) All my friends are completely bovine. I'm the only one with any spark about me.

Dream six

A purple baboon playing a lute started to sing a song about peeling onions, then it turned out to be the pharaoh, and I had to tell it what a wonderful singer it was.

Meaning:

a) I had too many figs to eat for supper.
b) I had too much cheese to eat for supper.
c) My uncle Merey is coming to stay. I can't stand him, but he's promised my family he'll pay for the repair of our roof and I've got to be nice to him.

What you eat, or indeed, what might eat you, are some of the many causes of unusual dreams.

ANSWERS

All the b's are the correct interpretations of the dreams, and are based on explanations found in the sacred Egyptian text *The Book of Dreams*.

Score 2 points for all answer b's. Score 1 point for all answer a's, and 0 points for all answer c's.

If you score between 9 and 12 – give yourself a big cheer and a pat on the back!

If you score between 6 and 8 – give yourself an indifferent shrug and say, "Phhh!"

If you score less than 6 – Give yourself a kick, and hiss like a snake!

What your answers say about you

Mostly a's. You are a highly practical person with little time for the spiritual world. Perhaps you should spend more time contemplating the afterlife.

Mostly b's. You are a very religious person in touch with the gods, and at one with the spiritual nature of the world.

Mostly c's. You are a hardened old cynic. Mend your ways or you'll be fed to a monster in the afterlife.

Ask Dr. Ahhk!

HE'S THE ECHO'S DOC ON THE SPOT

We all know a trip to the doctor's can be ruinously expensive. An ugly wound may be about to turn green, but if you haven't got those copper ingots, jars of figs, and three spare slaves to pay the doctor, then you'll just have to grin and bear it.

Until now. In another exclusive Echo readers' service, esteemed graduate of the famous medical academy of Per Bastet, Dr. Ahhkerkau (doctor of the Queen's toes and shepherd of the King's bottom) is AT YOUR SERVICE.

SMITTEN

Dear Dr. Ahhk,

Yesterday I was out smiting some Hittites. Some so-and-so slashed me with his sword and now I've got a nasty wound all down my arm. My dad splashed water over it, but it's still turned a lurid green. I can't afford some copper ingots, jars of figs and three spare slaves to pay my local doctor, and I'm afraid it might drop off, or worse. What can I do?

P. Tjebu, Tarkhan

Well P., that does sound nasty. Here is what you need to do. First of all cover the wound with a piece of fresh meat (stewing steak will do, you don't need to use best rump) and leave it there for one day. Then for the next few days you'll need to apply a daily fresh dressing of linen soaked in honey (and make sure it *is* changed every day). You may also like to pray fervently to the god Isis for a speedy recovery. Give it a week or so, get plenty of rest, and soon you will be as right as rain.

FOOLISH YOUTH

Dear Dr. Ahhk,

When I was a foolish youth and mixed with bad company, I shaved my head and had the words *KARNAK KOSH BOYS KICK TO KILL* tattooed across the top of my skull.

I am now 35 and have a prestigious job as a government tax inspector. Alas, I am also going bald. Every morning brings fresh horror. Please help, I am desperate.

J. Hatibi, Karnak.

Many patients come to me with worries about baldness, and I am pleased to tell you there is a quick and easy solution. Take one freshly dead crow (a chariot kill would do), remove one of its vertebra and crush to a fine powder. Sprinkle a smidgen of burned asses hoof over it, mix together with a dollop of black snake lard, and bake at 200°C (420°F) for twenty minutes. Rub gently into the affected area while the potion is still warm, but for Amun's sake DON'T EAT IT. Alternatively, you may wish to purchase a wig.

CROCODILE TEARS

Dear Dr. Ahhk,

Me and my friends want to take a river trip from el-Amarna to Aswan. I'd love to go but I'm petrified of being eaten by a crocodile, not to mention being stung by a scorpion, or bitten by a snake. My friends say an accident like this is highly unlikely, but I'm not so sure, and keep dreaming about huge gaping jaws and grinding teeth. What can I do?

W. Qedes, el-Amarna

Well W., you are a sissy. I have known lots of people who have been eaten by crocodiles, and it doesn't hurt that much. However, there is a sure-fire cure to your problems. You need to buy a stone amulet with the image of Horus the god wrestling with a crocodile, snake or scorpion engraved upon it. (These are available from *Godz 4 Uz*, *Nofret's Niknaks*, and all good amulet stores. Ask for the *Horus bite-guard*©® brands.) Pour water over the amulet, drink the drops that flow from it, and voilà – your safety is guaranteed.

Be sure to obtain a separate amulet depicting Horus wrestling with each of the animals you wish to gain protection from. Have a nice trip!

WHAT'S BEEN GOING ON HERE?

Dear Dr. Ahhk,

I woke up recently with severe back pains, and I've been having recurring headaches that last for days. My tongue has taken on an unpleasant yellowy coating and I also have several other symptoms unsuitable for a family newspaper such as this. What do you reckon?

R. Paheri, Panopolis.

I shall tell you what I reckon, Mr. R. Peheri of 23 Naga el-Deir Road, Panopolis, I reckon you have been up to NO GOOD, and the god Osiris has sent a demon to torment you. Perhaps you have been "seeing" your friend's wife, or pilfering grain from the village stores? Whatever it is, I would suggest you STOP DOING IT IMMEDIATELY.

THIS WEEK'S STAR LETTER

WORM TROUBLE

Dear Dr. Ahhk,

I have a terrible toothache that's been keeping me awake all night. I've tried to treat it with cloves and olive oil, a hot poultice, and prayers and offerings to the great god Ma'at. Alas, nothing seems to work. What do you suggest?

P. Pepyankh (Mrs.), Naqada.

Bad luck Mrs. P., you have what we doctors call a *fenet worm* gnawing away at your tooth. You probably contracted the worm by eating some bad food.

These worms are the cause of many common ailments. They need to be driven out of the body as quickly as possible by the ingestion of foul potions. What you need to do is mix up an utterly repellent mixture of rotten vegetables, horse manure, jackal blood and mud from the banks of the Nile and then eat it three times a day. Wash it down with a glass of water, and avoid alcohol for the duration of the treatment. It's not a very nice remedy, but believe me, "Doctor knows best!" Keep at it for a week and it should do the trick!

You can write to Dr. Ahhkerkau at **The EGYPTIAN ECHO**, Pyramid Row, Memphis

YOUR **ECHO** GUARANTEE OF GOOD HEALTH

Dr. Ahhkerkau only uses cures and remedies that are at least 1,000 years old, and are guaranteed to come from tried and trusted sacred texts. Nevertheless neither the **EGYPTIAN ECHO** nor Dr. Ahhkerkau himself accepts any responsibility for fatalities or further injuries occurring to readers following advice offered in these pages.

Dr. Ahhkerkau regrets he is unable to enter into personal correspondence with **ECHO** readers.

Would YOU like to

- **portray the power of a proud and noble ruler?**
- **depict the poise of a gracious lady?**
- **evoke the startled stare of a man roused from sleep?**

Let ME show YOU how!

Khun Anup, painter at the palace library of sacred books, offers you the chance to join his famous painting and drawing course. This could enable you to get a job in the royal workshop, or as a tomb artist where you can guarantee your patron's immortality by painting an accurate likeness of him on the walls of his tomb.

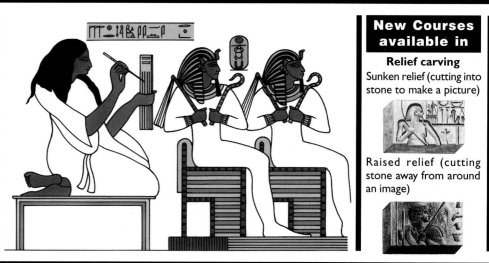

New Courses available in

Relief carving
Sunken relief (cutting into stone to make a picture)

Raised relief (cutting stone away from around an image)

Some of the skills you'll learn on Khun's course

FORM AND CONVENTION

Who's the most important person in this picture? That's right, it's him in the middle. You can tell, as he's the biggest, followed by his wife, and his children. Servants are shown smallest of all.

Get this wrong, and you're in BIG TROUBLE!

EGYPTIAN PERSPECTIVE

Look at this table...

Wrong

You can't see what's on it from just one angle.

Right

That's better – now everything on the table can be seen.

It's especially important to master this technique for paintings on tomb walls, as the spirit of the deceased will be able to make use of all the items you depict.

THE MEANING OF THE PAINTS AT YOUR DISPOSAL –

White – for luxury and joy
Bright yellow – for gods' bodies
Pale yellow – for women's faces
Brown-red – for men's faces
Red – for evil and violence
Green – for water and youth
Blue – for the hair of gods
Black – for the earth

HOW TO MIX YOUR PAINTS

How to take simple materials such as earth, chalk, charcoal and soot, and mix them with other minerals and water, acacia tree gum and egg white to make almost any shade you like.

THE STRICT RULES YOU MUST ADHERE TO IN FIGURE ILLUSTRATION

Proportion
Figures can be drawn on a grid of 20 or so squares. There are strict rules about what goes where. For example the length of a forearm must **always** be three squares.

Perspective
The idea here is to show as much of the body as possible, without completely distorting the picture. The face is always in profile, but with the eye in full view. The torso is always seen from the front, but the lower body and legs from the side, with both legs showing.

Look at me, I turned my talent into fame and fortune. Stand above the common herd – status, wealth, and work satisfaction await. So what are you waiting for – SIGN UP NOW!!

Khun Anup
Palace View Avenue
Memphis

ART FOR ATEN'S SAKE

Art
WATCH

Art-shock controversy for god-swap Akhe

The world of Egyptian art has been shaken to its very foundations by Pharaoh Akhenaten. Not content with telling everyone they can't worship the traditional deities of Egypt, the god-swap pharaoh has also turned the world of art upside down. **OUT** go stiff and formal portraits of the royal family, and depictions of the pharaoh as strong and handsome. **IN** come cheerful family scenes and warts-and-all depictions of the royal countenance.

Spark

The spark that set the bushfires of artistic controversy blazing is a new portrait of the royal family, unveiled yesterday.

In a raised stone relief the Pharaoh is shown with his wife Nefertiti and three of his young daughters. Baby Ankhesenpaaten **plays** with Queen Nefertiti's crown. Meketaten **perches** on her mother's knee. King Akhenaten **kisses** daughter Meritaten.

Flagrant

This scene of flagrantly carefree family life has sent shockwaves reverberating through the dignified world of Egyptian art, which is quite unused to such outrageous informality. Royal observers are especially startled by the fact that Nefertiti is even **sitting on Akhenaten's throne!**

The portrait that shocked a nation. Many feel kissing babies is rather undignified.

FAYOUM FEVER HITS ASWAN

Egypt's top music sensation, the Fayoum Four (featuring Fazzy Flute), are wowing the nation with their latest creation *Spend the day merrily (put ointment and fine oil to your nostrils).* **Guests who flocked to see them at a wedding in** Aswan were treated to a two hour show by the near-naked quartet.

Currently on a tour of public festivals, parties and funeral ceremonies, the four are stunning audiences with their daring mixture of traditional Egyptian pipes and harps, and the latest flutes, lyres and lutes from Asia.

Smirk

Fazzy, 23, (real name Tefnakhte Mengebet) whose first public performance was playing to sweaty Nile Delta farm hands, has been romantically linked with Egypt's top juggler, Koptos. "We're just good friends," she smirked when questioned by reporters gathered at the show.

Noise

But village elders were unimpressed with the quartet. "You can't hear the words," said one. "And the music – it's just a noise."

A young fan (middle) rushes the stage as the flute, lute, harp and lyre quartet wow Aswan revellers.

DO THE HIPPO HIPPO SHAKE

A new dance is sweeping the country. Named after Egypt's sacred and much loved hippopotamus, the "hippo hippo shake" is a hip grinding, leg swirling, arm whirling sensation!

Cut it out

Just follow our cut-out-and-keep guide and you can't go wrong!

For you older "hippos" this dance can be a superb exercise routine to tone up those flabby muscles and burn off those extra calories. (Be sure to consult your doctor before embarking on any strenuous exercise, says the Echo's legal consultant!)

DO THE HIPPO HIPPO SHAKE

DANCE GUIDE

1. You shake your hips to the left...

2. ...put your leg up in the air.

3. You shake your hips to the right...

4. ...wave your arms like you don't care.

(Lyric reproduced by kind permission of Tefnakhte Mengebet/Memphis Music)

HEY, LET'S

Throw the party of your life with the Echo's B to Z guide to faultless entertaining

The long, light evenings are upon us and 'tis the season to be MERRY. Parties can be great fun, but they're also a handy way of impressing your boss, making your rivals look like cheapskates, and letting your relatives and friends know you're a successful, pretty powerful kind of guy.

Here's the Echo's **B** to **Z** guide to how to have the most FANTASTIC PARTY OF YOUR LIFE.

 is for **B**EER. You'll need plenty of this, and wine, to make your party go with a swing. But remember "wine and beer make you feel queer" – so don't mix the two!

It also stands for **B**OREDOM. Be on the lookout for drooping eyes, and for that deadly moment when stifled yawns replace lively conversation. You'll need to act fast to pep things up, and bring on the musicians or the acrobats immediately.

 is for **D**ANCING. Not for your guests of course – no one would expect guests to dance at a party, but you'll need to hire some dancers to entertain your guests with a few pirouettes, when they've had enough food and gossip.

is for **F**LATTERY. Be sure to have a good range of outrageous compliments at the ready, so guests can admire your eloquence. **Do say** things like "Thou art secure and thine enemies are brought low!", and "Thou enterest into the presence of the Divine Judges, and thou cometh forth in triumph!" **Don't say** things like "Thou art not nearly as bad as people say thou art!" or "For a man of fifty, thou could be a lot fatter than thou art!"

It also stands for **F**LOWERS. Make sure every guest has a lotus flower to admire or sniff discreetly if the occasion demands it (see **I**.)

 is for **G**OLD and silver cups and plates. There's no point trying to impress your guests with wonderful food and drink if you're going to serve it on palm leaves and clay cups. Remember IF YOU'VE GOT IT, FLAUNT IT.

is for **H**ARPS. We all like music, and what better accompaniment to the merry tinkle of conversation than the merry tinkle of a tasteful harp.

is for **I**NCAPACITATED. Don't worry about your guests being sick – it just means they're HAVING A GOOD TIME. Be sure your servants have plenty of fresh water and towels to cope with those "little accidents".

is for "**J**UST ENOUGH IS NEVER ENOUGH". The whole point of a party is to get so thoroughly stuffed you put on three chins, and don't want to eat again for a MONTH!

The more roast ox, goose, catfish and mullet you provide the better, along with enough drinks to drown a boatload of baboons.

PAAAARTY!!

Can you spot which of these lovely ladies is about to see her dinner again? Bring water immediately!!

 is for **KARNAK, KHNEMHOTEP II, KIDNEY BEANS, KALEIDOSCOPE, KARAOKE, KILLER BEES**, and absolutely <u>NO WORDS AT ALL</u> to do with parties and entertaining in Ancient Egypt!

is for **MUSICIANS**. As well as playing discreetly in the background, you'll also need music to accompany your dancers. The more musicians the merrier – a quartet at least.

It's become fashionable for musicians to sing about what a great time everybody is having, or to point out that their glasses are empty and they ought to drink more wine.

is for **NIBBLES**. Quaint little delicacies are just what you need when you've stuffed your face with ox and duck. Be sure to have a good supply of figs, dates and tasty little honeyed pastries.

is for **PRAISES** heaped upon the host. It is quite acceptable to instruct your hired musicians to sing about what a splendid fellow you are.

Who knows? Maybe the message will seep in!

is for **QUEEN OF PUDDINGS** – a wonderful mixture of bread, custard, jam and meringue, unfortunately unknown to us Ancient Egyptians.

is for **RECEIVING GUESTS**. If someone really important is coming, you must make a great show of being at the door to greet them as they arrive. Not only is this good manners, but it also allows the slobs next door, and your surly employees or farmhands to see you hobnobbing with royalty or similar posh people. You can greet lesser mortals in your reception room. Be sure to look down your nose at them, but don't snigger or sneer unless you really can't help it.

is for **SEATING**. Make sure you have the most important seat in the dining room – it's your party after all.

If you have someone TITANICALLY important as a guest it's best to offer them a seat of similar elaborateness (people have been ruined for less). Guests of similar status should be seated around you.

If your party is very formal then men and women should sit separately. If it is informal, then husbands and wives may sit together if they so wish.

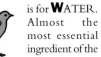 is for **SHAMBLES** – which is what your house will look like after the party.

is for **TRANSPARENT CLOTHING**. Your servants, dancers and musicians should all wear revealing clothing, or even better, NOTHING AT ALL. In the future people will get really indignant about this sort of thing, so MAKE THE MOST OF IT NOW!

is for **"TSH**!! Just look at old Harkhuf over there, eyeing up Miss Nebankh. Chubby middle-aged men aren't really her type."

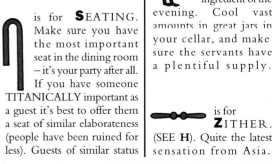 is for **WATER**. Almost the most essential ingredient of the evening. Cool vast amounts in great jars in your cellar, and make sure the servants have a plentiful supply.

is for **ZITHER**. (SEE **H**). Quite the latest sensation from Asia.

Uncle Amen's topmost tip

Grill or bake?

Uncle Amen pouring oil on troubled waters.

Drunken baboon

Dear Uncle Amen,

I am so completely in love with this girl in our street that it's making me dizzier than a drunken baboon. Her hair is blacker than the night, her lips are redder than ripe dates, her voice is softer than a tinkling harp (*Yes, yes, get on with it – Uncle Amen*). Unfortunately, her family is much richer than mine and she won't even LOOK at me, never mind let me marry her.

Every night I lie awake dreaming of the day we can meet and rub noses, and I can tell the whole world she's mine forever. What can I do?

K.A., Memphis

Pull yourself together K. – everyone in Egypt has black hair, and most people have red lips, unless they're suffering from a particularly unpleasant ailment. Granted, not every girl has a voice like a tinkling harp, but <u>really</u>, she doesn't sound THAT special. Anyway, here is my advice;

> **Do not make a ferry on the river, and then strain to seek its fare.**
> **Take the fare from him who is wealthy, and let pass him who is poor.**
> **The gods prefer him who reveres the poor to him who worships the wealthy.**

Now, isn't that a comfort?

Upset? A problem aired is a problem shared. The Echo's agony columnist "Uncle" Amenemope is at your service, with kind words and comforting advice to help restore your inner harmony. Just write away to

Dear Uncle Amen

Son is a scamp

Dear Uncle Amen,

We were so proud when our son went off to medical school at Per Bastet, but now his tutors write to us with terrible news. They say he neglects his pen and papyrus to abandon himself to dancing, drinking and consorting with all sorts of scamps and scallywags. Instead of studying the workings of the human heart and its attendant valves and channels, he frightens people in the street, lurching from one beer hall to another.

What can we do?

K.P., Luxor

Your son has strayed further into the abyss than a cat into a herd of basking crocodiles. His heart must be denser than a great obelisk. Try not to fret, and in the meantime you may like to reflect on this advice:

> **Do not say 'Today is like tomorrow' How will this end? Comes tomorrow, today has vanished. The deep has become the water's edge.**

There, isn't that better?

Inde-*scribe*-able

Dear Uncle Amen,

My younger brother is training to be a scribe, and he's turned into the snootiest, cockiest little twerp this side of the fertile crescent. He keeps turning his nose up at me and says "I'm going to have the best job in the world, unlike you, a mere sailor, who might go to sea and be devoured by a storm, and unlike brother Rensi, who spends his days bending over in the boiling sun, toiling in the fields, and comes home stinking and exhausted."

What can I do to bring him down to earth?

B.N., Thebes

Dear Uncle Amen,

Please can you settle an argument that is bringing much discord to our household. I insist that the best way to cook mullet is to grill it with a knob of butter. My mother-in-law however, insists that baking it wrapped in palm leaves with garlic and onions, is by far the best way. The old bat beats me with a stick when I do it my way, and my husband just looks the other way and pretends nothing is happening.

What do you think?

P.K., Abydos

Between you and me I always say why go to the bother of stoking up an oven when you can grill over an open fire. Most fish taste the same whatever you do with them, so I'm with you on the fish question. However, reading between the lines, I detect a far more serious issue here than how to cook fish. Respect for elders is one of the fundamental cornerstones of our society, and you do seem to be rather lacking in it. Perhaps you would like to think about this:

> **Do not revile one older than you for she shall see the gods before you.**
> **Let her not report you to them saying "My daughter -in-law hath reviled me"**
> **Remember – A dog's food is from its master, it barks to him who gives it.**

Do I detect a hint of jealousy here B.? Alas, your pestilent brother is right, and your sourness will make you disagreeable in the eyes of your family. I say to you:

> **Guard your tongue from harmful speech, then you will be loved by others.**

You could console yourself by thinking he may end up spending his days counting jars of grain in a warehouse, while you yourself are enjoying the blessings of bracing breezes and plenty of sunshine. In the meantime, try and be nice to him – as a scribe he'll almost certainly end up as an influential, wealthy individual.

Goose in a whirlpool

Dear Uncle Amen,

I am so completely in love with this boy in our street that it's making me dizzier than a goose in a whirlpool. His hair is blacker than sloes. His lips are redder than beads of red jasper, and his voice is stronger than the roar of a ferocious crocodile.

Unfortunately he is already married, and he won't even LOOK at me, never mind anything else. Every night I wander in the garden, whispering my love to the flowers and the birds, and I dream of a day when we can walk together along the banks of the Nile, arm in arm.

A.R., Thebes

Well A, you are tottering on the brink of a deep ravine. If this fellow begins to think your hair is blacker than a very black blackcurrant, and your lips are redder than a very red redcurrant (let's assume he's not much of a poet) and wants to start seeing you too, then you'll be in bigger trouble than a camel in a snow storm. In fact, being a camel in a snow storm would be considerably better than being stoned to death, and then having your remains fed to wild dogs, which is what would happen if people found out about the two of you.

I offer you these words of advice…

> **Man is clay and straw, the god is his builder. He tears down, he builds up daily. Look at the bowl that is before you and let it serve your needs.**

*What you really need is a distraction. I'm sending you the address of K.A. in Memphis (see **Drunken Baboon**, above) He sounds like a nice boy, and he also seems to be at a loose end. Perhaps you could get in touch?*

 ★ Note to scholars. These translations of *Amenemope's Instructions* are taken from Miriam Lichtheim's *Ancient Egyptian Literature* Three volumes ©1973-1980 Regents of the University of California.

• Pets corner • Pets corner • Pets corner •

Pet Geese?
YOU MUST BE HONKERS!

If Old Macdonald lived in Egypt, he would have kept geese in the house as well as on that farm.

Geese. We all like to eat them, but would YOU keep one as a PET? This idea isn't as fowl as it seems. Its plucky character and funny little ways have enabled the Nile goose to waddle into the hearts of householders throughout Egypt. It is allowed to paddle around the garden and even roam around inside the house.

Dog doesn't mind

Does the family dog seem to mind? Not a bit of it, and although geese don't get along so well with other popular household pets such as cats and monkeys, this mutual antagonism rarely stretches to more than the odd nip or squawk.

But best of all, say owners, a goose will keep burglars out of your house just as well as any guard dog, and it's far less fussy about its food.

Nine things you probably never knew about geese

❶ Rather disappointingly, a goose does not lay its eggs under a gooseberry bush.

❷ Despite its name the goose cannot do the goose step.

❸ In a fight between a cat and a goose, the cat will usually come off worse, unless it is especially fat and vicious.

❹ Geese cannot be trained to hunt crocodiles.

❺ A "dressed goose" is not one all done up for a night on the town – it's more likely to be one all done up for a few hours in the oven.

❻ Like us, geese have their own language. Because it has only two words – *honk* and *hssss* – it is especially easy to learn.

❼ Scholars think honk means "Hey, you there!!"

❽ They are less sure about hssss, but think it probably means "Get out of my way".

❾ Perhaps because of their limited vocabulary, there have been no great geese poets.

Animal laughs

Embalmer: "Would you like your cats turned into mummies, Madame?" Lady:"On no, Mister. They're both Toms – I'll just have them stuffed."

Hyena: "OK, act friendly, and let him stroke you. Then wait 'til his back's turned, and we'll steal the chickens!!"

CATS – JUST HOW SACRED ARE THEY?

We may have tried and failed to make a pet out of the hyena, but we certainly succeeded with the cat. In fact, historians tell us that Egypt was the first place on Earth where cats became household pets.

When the humble African wild cat moved out of the marshes and into our houses, it quickly became Egypt's most adored animal.

Owns the place

It may act like it owns the place, and walks off in a haughty sulk when you turf it out of your chair, but many people believe that cats (or *miu* as they're known in Egypt) are actually sacred! Here's why ...

★ Bastet, the goddess of happiness, likes cats so much she even looks like a cat.

★ If you make certain prayers and spells over a cat, the spirit of Bastet will enter it. Bastet can indicate her feelings toward you through the cat's actions. For example if it licks your hand then Bastet is pleased with you. If it takes a lump out of your arm with its claws then you're in serious trouble.

★ When a cat dies the household where it lives goes into mourning, and everyone shaves their eyebrows. You wouldn't do that for any old animal would you?

Miu loves yah? We do!

WIN THIS BOAT!

A chariot may be quite Hyksosian, a horse on its own will save your feet, but everyone agrees (from godly kings to buzzing bees), that a boat upon the Nile is quite a treat!

So wrote Egypt's top songwriter Fazzy Flute in her hymn of praise to our greatest asset – the wonderful Nile river. To celebrate the beginning of the season of Akhet, when the Nile floods its banks and irrigates our fields, we're GIVING AWAY this magnificent deluxe sailing vessel.

All you have to do is answer the following 20 questions, and send them to us by the first day of the third week of the first month of Akhet, 1334BC. The first correct entry to be pulled from our bag will WIN THIS BOAT.

No cheating now!

The ECHO's fabulous Akhet season contest offers you the chance to GO BOATING IN STYLE!!

Just look at these features:

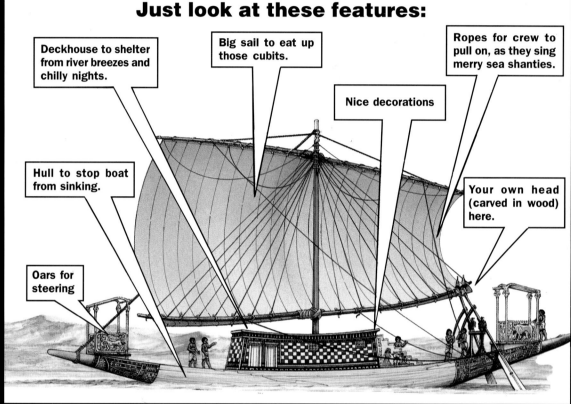

Deckhouse to shelter from river breezes and chilly nights.

Big sail to eat up those cubits.

Ropes for crew to pull on, as they sing merry sea shanties.

Nice decorations

Hull to stop boat from sinking.

Your own head (carved in wood) here.

Oars for steering

TWENTY QUIZZICAL QUESTIONS

1) What did Ramesses III do to the Sea People?
a) bought them all ice cream; b) smote them good and proper;
c) sold them chariot insurance.

2) Which sacred pet likes to have mice for lunch?

3) Thilly thothage or divine intellectual thenthation?

4) What do you see in your dreams?
a) the future; b) the past; c) the present.

5) Hrglyphcs dnt hv ths...

6) Egyptian civilization (not to mention our floods, boats and crocodiles) would never have happened without which river?

7) Ancient Egyptians add up to 10,000 with one of these:
a) severed finger;
b) flowery squiggle;
c) sun-powered pocket calculator.

8) This royal he was really a she!

9) Big pointy-topped things where pharaohs were buried, which were made with millions of limestone blocks, and built by 100,000 workers.

10) Fashionable headwear for sweet-smelling parties:
a) hollowed-out crocodile head; b) perfumed fat cone; c) miner's hat with built-in torch.

11) Sun god who was eclipsed during the reign of King Tut.

12) This Egyptian capital was named after a city in Tennessee, USA – or was it

the other way around?

13) Which flying ingredient is part of a cure for baldness? Is it:

a) the pilot's seat from a Boeing 747 (boiled and diced); b) the vertebra of a crow (crushed); c) the iron head on the tip of an arrow (melted).

14) Urns for your organs.

15) They kept the Hyksos awake with their bellowing.

16) You might have this cut off for stealing a shepherd.

17) It waddles, lays eggs, says honk and hiss, and you can eat it.

18) A marsh reed which is essential for writing.

19) They were Egypt's first invaders.

20) Workers on Ramesses III's tomb went on strike because:
a) they wanted to watch a football match; b) they wanted to bring down the government; c) they hadn't been paid their wages.